Fairwood PTSA

Thank you for donating this
book in support of the
writing program.

My Story by
Francis the Bird

with help from
Carla C. Cain

Fairwood Elem. School
16600 148th Ave. S. E.
Renton, WA 98058

F.S. Press

LIBRARY OF CONGRESS CATALOGING-IN-PUBLICATION DATA
Cain, Carla, date-
My Story by Francis the Bird/ by Carla C. Cain

Summary: A newborn sparrow falls from its nest and is rescued by a girl who raises him until he "leaves the nest".

(1. Birds-Fiction. 2. Animal babies.)   (E)-dc22   2003098763

ISBN 0-9717088-0-0   (hardcover)

Printed in the United States of America

First edition: April 2004

www.francisthebird.com

Photographs and design:
Carla C. Cain

F.S. Press

This story is dedicated to Monica,
Matthew, Braydon, and Lani.
May your hearts remain tender
and your kindness bright.

We have been called upon to heal wounds, to unite what has fallen apart, and to bring home those who have lost their way -

St. Francis

SPLAT!

was the sound I made when I fell all
the way from my nest to the
hard rocks below.

I didn't know what to do so I did the
only thing I was good at back then–

I SCREAMED!!!

I opened my big, yellow, clown-like
lips and screamed as loud as I could!

Suddenly I was going back up into
the sky, but this time I was safe in
the hands of one of the giant
things that have wings but
cannot fly.

The giant fed me and held me close.
Soon I was very drowsy and
drifted off to sleep.

I quickly settled into my new home
with my giant girl. She
was my friend.

She tucked me into a basket and took
me everywhere she went. She took
me to a lake once to show me
a pretty sunset.

Sometimes I peeked up over the top
of the basket to see the world...

then I ducked down and hid because
the world looked way too
scary for me!

While I was under the covers I
pretended I was flying.

I flapped my wings as hard as I could
but never left the ground.

Sometimes I flapped myself to sleep.

I grew real fast.

Before I knew it, I had a full set of
wings. My girl put a mirror
in my basket so that I
could admire them.

I tried them out, but they were
mostly for looks. When I
tried to fly and crashed,

my girl would rub my tummy and
tell me how proud of me she was.
Sometimes I pretended to be an
eagle just to make her laugh!

Every night she wrapped me in my
blanket and laid me in her lap.

We stared at each other until I
fell asleep and dreamed
of flying.

Then one day I thought I was big
enough to leave the nest.

"Can I? Can I, huh?" I asked my girl.
We went outside...

Fairwood Elem. School
16600 148th Ave. S. E.
Renton, WA 98058

I am now almost grown. I can fly from
rooftop to treetop and back again.
I show off for my girl when she
comes out to see me.

When she calls my name I answer and
soar down to sit on her shoulder.
Some day when she is older and
her feathers come in, I will
teach her how to fly and
we will fly together.

-the end